Benny McGee and the SHARK

THE SHARK REPORT

For Lyle—the real Mr. Fitzgerald,
who taught me to swim

PENGUIN WORKSHOP
An Imprint of Penguin Random House LLC, New York

The publisher does not have any control over and does not assume any responsibility
for author or third-party websites or their content.

Copyright © 2020 by Derek Anderson. All rights reserved. Published by
Penguin Workshop, an imprint of Penguin Random House LLC, New York.
PENGUIN and PENGUIN WORKSHOP are trademarks of Penguin Books Ltd,
and the W colophon is a registered trademark of Penguin Random House LLC.
Manufactured in China.

Visit us online at www.penguinrandomhouse.com.

Library of Congress Cataloging-in-Publication Data is available upon request.

ISBN 9780593093399 (paperback)   10 9 8 7 6 5 4 3 2 1
ISBN 9780593093382 (library binding)   10 9 8 7 6 5 4 3 2 1

Benny McGee
and the
SHARK

THE
SHARK
REPORT

by Derek Anderson

Penguin Workshop

CHAPTER ONE

"Come in and swim, Benny," called my dad. "The water feels great!"

Was he crazy? I knew I could never go swimming again.

There might be a shark in that water.

I know all about sharks.

We're studying the ocean and its creatures at school.

My teacher, Mr. Fitzgerald, is making us write reports about them.

Mr. Fitzgerald even invited a deep-sea fisherman to our class next week to tell us about all the things he has seen. I wonder if he has ever seen a real shark.

"I don't know what you're so afraid of," said my dad as we gathered our things to go home that afternoon.

I wasn't listening, though. I was busy looking behind us.

I was pretty sure we were being followed.

CHAPTER TWO

I had that same funny feeling the next morning when I left for school.

Something wasn't right.

It was raining pretty hard by the time I turned onto Anchor Street.

That's when I saw him—a giant shark!

I tried not to worry.

Mr. Fitzgerald said some sharks only eat plankton, which has a lot of plants in it.

I hoped this one was looking for a salad.

When I wiped the rain out of my eyes, I could see better.

This was not my lucky day.

He was a great white.

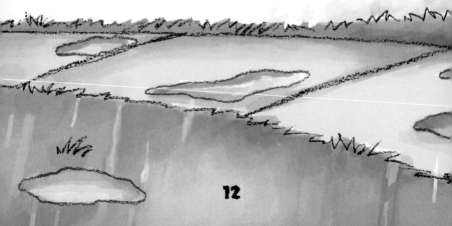

I tried not to freak out.
That lasted seven seconds.
Then I made a break for it.

I have never run faster.
Mr. Fitzgerald told us great
whites don't travel in schools.

Luckily for me, I was only a block
from my school, so I knew I would be
safe once I got inside.

After we did all our math
problems, I checked the playground.
I couldn't see the shark anywhere.
He was probably hiding.

Mr. Fitzgerald said sharks like to surprise their prey.

I liked surprises, but not *that* kind.

I didn't want to be anybody's afternoon snack.

So, after school, I ran home.

CHAPTER THREE

I made it home in record time.

As soon as I got inside,
I remembered how Mr. Fitzgerald
said sharks like to circle their food
while they decide if it looks tasty.

I must have left my scooter in the
yard, because the shark started
riding it around our house.

On his third time around, I knew.
He was circling me.

I hurried into the office and told
my mom about the shark.

"He's probably lost," she said.

Then I told my dad.

"He might need water. Why don't you let him in," he said.

Let him in? My dad had lost his marbles.

Mr. Fitzgerald said sharks don't eat people very often.

He said I had a better chance of winning a million dollars than being eaten by a shark.

I had never won anything, so I figured I'd be safe.

I took a deep breath and let him in.

CHAPTER FOUR

I gave the shark a glass of water.

He slurped it down, so I gave him another.

Then I accidentally handed him a glass of water with ice in it.

After that, he wouldn't drink anything *without* ice.

I didn't know sharks were so picky!

I decided to call him Mr. Chompers because of his big teeth.

He seemed to like that name.

My teacher knows a lot about sharks.

But I learned things that even Mr. Fitzgerald doesn't know.

Like how sharks are terrible at playing fetch.

Mr. Chompers chased the balls when I threw them—but then he ate them. All of them!

A shark will eat almost anything.
Even that weird meat loaf my dad
fixed for dinner.

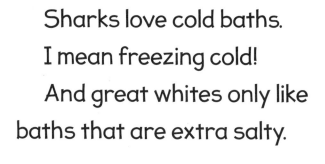

Sharks love cold baths.
I mean freezing cold!
And great whites only like
baths that are extra salty.

I kind of liked having Mr. Chompers around.

I never thought a shark would be fun to hang out with, but I was learning all sorts of new things. And then it hit me—my report!

My shark report was due in the morning. It was almost bedtime, and I hadn't even started writing it!

Then I got the perfect idea.

CHAPTER FIVE

I didn't need to write a report. I could bring Mr. Chompers to school instead!

Everybody would flip if they saw me walk in with a great white shark.

I'd be a hero. Mr. Fitzgerald would probably give me some kind of medal.

First, we'd have to get through the night. I didn't know anything about how sharks sleep.

I found that out the hard way.

I made up a place for Mr. Chompers on the floor in my room, but he wouldn't lie down.

It turns out that great whites keep moving, even while they sleep.

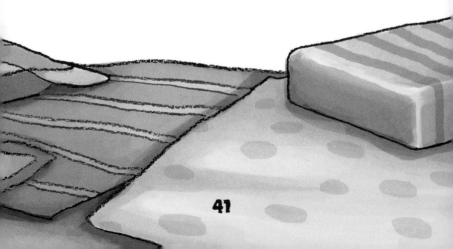

That goofy shark was wandering around my room with his eyes closed all night!

Every time he bumped into my desk or bed, or the wall, it woke me up.

It was a *very* long night.

The next morning, Mr. Chompers and I got ready for school.

He didn't have a toothbrush, so I let him use my dad's. It took forever. He used a whole tube of toothpaste. Sharks have a lot of teeth!

I told him to hurry. I couldn't wait to see everybody's faces when we walked in.

On the way to school, I told
Mr. Chompers that my class was
going to be excited to see him.

"But don't eat anybody!" I said.

That could really hurt my grade
on this report.

Just as we got to school, an old rusty truck pulled up and jerked to a stop. It was the deep-sea fisherman coming to speak to our class.

I had totally forgotten.

CHAPTER SIX

We had almost made it to the school when someone yelled, "SHARK!"

The fisherman reached into his truck and grabbed his net.

"NO!" I screamed. I turned to look at Mr. Chompers, but he'd already gone bounding down the street.

Without hesitating, I chased after him.

We had to get to the sea—it was
his only chance.

Mr. Fitzgerald said sharks are
really fast swimmers.

Sadly, they are terrible at running.

The fisherman was right on
Mr. Chompers's fins and my heels.

"Come here, you," growled
the fisherman.

That's when I remembered a
shortcut. "THIS WAY!" I screamed.

We turned down South Bay Street, dashed three more blocks, and cut through Mrs. Snodgrass's yard to the shore. Mr. Chompers was just about to leap in when I screamed, "*MR. CHOMPERS, WAIT!*"

He stopped and looked back at me.

"Will I ever see you again?" I asked.
Mr. Chompers wrapped his fins
around me and squeezed.

"GOTCHA!" yelled the fisherman,
and he hurled his net.

CHAPTER SEVEN

With a flip of his tail, Mr. Chompers plunged into the sea and disappeared beneath the waves. The net missed him by a split second.

The fisherman was sent to the principal's office for throwing his net at a student.

He got into a lot of trouble.

Since I hadn't written a report,
I didn't get a very good grade in
science. My class never got to see
Mr. Chompers, either.

And Mr. Fitzgerald didn't believe me when I told him all the things I'd learned about sharks—how they like ice in their drinks, they're terrible at playing fetch, they sleepwalk all night, and deep down, beneath their fins and teeth, they have big hearts.

But I know the truth.

And I will never be afraid to go swimming in the ocean again.

61

About the Author
by Benny McGee

Derek Anderson is pretty good at writing stories and drawing pictures, so I chose him to help me turn my story into a book. He didn't really do that much. I told him everything to write down.

Derek has made a lot of books: about ducks, a purple gorilla, a speedy hamster, a bunch of pigs, a goofy alligator and grumpy crocodile, and other cool things. I think this is his best book because it's about me and Mr. Chompers.

Derek lives in Minneapolis with his wife, Cheryl, and their dog, Louie. You can see more on his website: www.DerekAnderson.net.

COMING SOON:

Benny McGee
and the
SHARK

WE ARE
FAMOUS!